The Boy Who Walked on Air

BOOKS BY SCOTT CORBETT

The Trick Books
THE LEMONADE TRICK
THE MAILBOX TRICK
THE DISAPPEARING DOG TRICK
THE LIMERICK TRICK
THE BASEBALL TRICK
THE TURNABOUT TRICK
THE HAIRY HORROR TRICK
THE HATEFUL PLATEFUL TRICK
THE HOME RUN TRICK
THE HOCKEY TRICK

What Makes It Work?
WHAT MAKES A CAR GO?
WHAT MAKES TV WORK?
WHAT MAKES A LIGHT GO ON?
WHAT MAKES A PLANE FLY?
WHAT MAKES A BOAT FLOAT?

Suspense Stories
TREE HOUSE ISLAND
DEAD MAN'S LIGHT
CUTLASS ISLAND
ONE BY SEA
COP'S KID
THE BASEBALL BARGAIN
THE MYSTERY MAN
THE CASE OF THE GONE GOOSE
THE CASE OF THE FUGITIVE FIREBUG
THE CASE OF THE TICKLISH TOOTH
THE RED ROOM RIDDLE
DEAD BEFORE DOCKING
RUN FOR THE MONEY
THE CASE OF THE SILVER SKULL
HERE LIES THE BODY

Easy-to-Read Adventure
DR. MERLIN'S MAGIC SHOP
THE GREAT CUSTARD PIE PANIC
THE BOY WHO WALKED ON AIR

The Boy Who Walked on Air

by

SCOTT CORBETT

Illustrated by
ED PARKER

An Atlantic Monthly Press Book
Little, Brown and Company
BOSTON   TORONTO

FIRST EDITION

T 05/75

Library of Congress Cataloging in Publication Data

Corbett, Scott.
  The boy who walked on air.

  "An Atlantic Monthly Press book."
  SUMMARY: The adventures of Max who "could do almost
anything if he . . . tried hard enough."
  [1. Humorous stories] I. Parker, Edward
II. Title.
PZ7.C79938Bo   [Fic]   74-22426
ISBN 0-316-15723-6

ATLANTIC-LITTLE, BROWN BOOKS
ARE PUBLISHED BY
LITTLE, BROWN AND COMPANY
IN ASSOCIATION WITH
THE ATLANTIC MONTHLY PRESS

Published simultaneously in Canada
by Little, Brown & Company (Canada) Limited

PRINTED IN THE UNITED STATES OF AMERICA

For Tamara Lynn
Our newest grandniece

Max was tall and skinny. Only one thing about him was unusual. He had the most amazing will power in the world.

Will power is the power to think about something and make ourselves do it. Some people have more will power than others.

Max had the most! He could do almost anything if he thought about it hard enough, and tried hard enough.

His friend Morry was short and round and when it came to figuring things out, he was unusually smart.

One day they went to a science show.

It was all about the World of the Future.

What they liked best was a car. It floated a foot off the ground and moved on a cushion of air.

AMAZING AIR VEHICLE

When they left the show they were
still talking about how the car worked.

"I'll bet you can do that," said
Morry.

"I'll have to think about it," said Max.

Max was thinking hard. He was frowning and staring straight ahead. Sweat was trickling down his forehead.

Max began to take longer and longer steps. Morry had to trot to keep up with him.

Then Max seemed to float ahead a little with each step. He floated farther and farther. Finally he floated about ten feet before he came down.

"You've got it!" cried Morry.

"Yes," said Max.

Morry was not surprised. He knew how Max could use his will power. He knew Max could even do things he was afraid of — if he really wanted to do them.

But Morry was always the one who thought of what to do next.

"Try it again, Max," he said. "See if you can make yourself get off the ground and really walk on air."

Max thought about it hard. He took a deep breath and made a little jump into the air.

He moved his feet, trying to walk. Max stayed in the same place but his feet kept going. They went faster and faster until he lost his balance and fell onto the sidewalk.

Max sat up frowning.

"It's too slippery," he said. "I can't get anywhere."

"What you need is something to give you a push," said Morry. "Let's go to my house. Maybe we can think of something."

They were glad to find nobody home at Morry's house. Max's strange power was a secret and they were careful to keep it a secret. Max never showed off in front of other people.

He sat on the edge of a chair while Morry raced upstairs. In a few minutes he was back with a large round fan with a wooden handle. It had a Japanese picture printed on it.

"My Aunt Mary sent this to my mother," said Morry. "If you fan the air very hard with it, I'll bet it will push you."

"But if I fan the air in front of me, it will make me go backwards," said Max.

"Don't worry about that. Just try it.
Then we'll figure out a way to make
you go forward."

"Well . . ." Max did not look too sure about this, but he took the fan.

"Ready? said Morry.

Max thought hard, getting his will power going, and then said, "Yes."

He hopped up into the air and started fanning as hard as he could.

He moved slowly backwards, a foot above the floor. He started swinging his feet back and forth, and he went faster. Much faster.

"Take it easy!" cried Morry, but it was too late. Max moved so fast he went all the way across the room. He

crashed against the wall and fell in a heap on the floor. He hit it so hard he knocked a small picture off the wall. The picture hit him on the head.

Morry hurried over and picked up the picture.

"Hey, we're lucky!" he said. "It didn't break."

"Some luck!" grumbled Max, rubbing his scalp. "What about my head?"

"It was only a small picture," said Morry. "Let's try something else. You need to see where you're going."

"I sure do!" said Max. "And I need more space!"

"Wait a minute, I've got another idea."

This time Morry went down to the basement. He came back carrying a limp air mattress and a bicycle pump.

"I'll blow it up," he said. "It will be ready in a minute."

Max watched nervously as Morry pumped.

"Ready for what?" he asked.

"To pull you along," said Morry.
"I'll hold the mattress up off the floor.
You grab hold of the edge of it. When
you jump, I'll pull the plug. The air will
rush out and you'll move like a jet
plane."

"It sounds crazy," said Max.

"It isn't. Trust me," said Morry.
"Come out on the back porch where
you'll have more room."

Max looked at the back yard. It was covered with snow, and one big snowdrift.

"Well," he said, "I don't know . . ."

"You had better start up here on the porch, Max," said Morry. "You can't get a good start if you stand in the snow. Don't worry! You can't hurt yourself. Even if you crash you'll land on nice soft snow."

"You're not doing the falling," said Max. "I'll try it, but just this once."

"That's the spirit!" said Morry.

21

Max frowned and sweated and worked up his will power. Morry held the air mattress up at shoulder height.

"Ready?"

"Here goes!" cried Max.

He gave a little hop into the air, grabbed the edge of the mattress, and started running while Morry pulled the plug.

There was only one thing wrong
with Morry's idea.

As the jet of air whooshed out of the
tube, it made the air mattress spin.
    With his legs flying, Max shot
across the back yard in circles. The
circles got smaller and faster until

finally Max and the mattress plunged
into the snowdrift. Max ended up with
his head and shoulders buried in snow
and his feet still running helplessly.

Morry pulled him out.

"Darn!" he said. "There must be a better way."

"I hope so!" said Max, spitting out a mouthful of snow.

Morry snapped his fingers. "I have a great idea!" he said.

"Never mind!" said Max. "I don't want any more —"

But Morry went right on talking.

"What you need is rockets, Max! And I have just the things!"

"Oh, no," said Max, looking worried.

"Just wait till I get them," said Morry.

He hurried into the house and came back with two cardboard tubes about a foot long and two big balloons.

He stretched the neck of a balloon over one of the tubes and blew up the balloon through the tube. The balloon grew larger than a beach ball and still larger. When Morry's face was bright red, he held his thumb over the end of the tube to keep the air inside the balloon.

"Here, take this," he said. "Keep the air in it with your thumb while I blow up the other balloon."

He blew and blew until finally the other balloon was full. Then he handed it to Max.

"Now, twist them around so that the tubes are pointing backwards. After you get off the ground take your thumbs off the ends," said Morry. "Then you will have two jets of air pushing you forward, just like a jet plane."

"Wow! Are you sure it will work?"

"It can't miss!"

"All right," said Max. "I'll try this once, but —"

"Ready?"

Max twisted the tubes around so that they were pointing backwards, gave a little running jump, and said, "Yes!"

"Go!" said Morry.

Max lifted himself off the ground, took his thumbs off the ends of the tubes, and walked.

This time he moved straight ahead
over the snow. Air hissed out of the
tubes in twin jets. His feet moved faster
and faster, and this time he went all the
way across the back yard, straight for a
big oak tree.

"Oh, help!" cried Max.

"Drop them!" cried Morry.

Max dropped the balloon rockets
and they fizzled away across the yard.
Max hit the tree.

"Hey, that was great!" said Morry,
plowing through the snow toward him.
Max sat up, shaking his head.

"Was it?" he said.

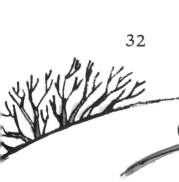

"Yes! But we need more room."

"We certainly do!"

"I know what to do!" said Morry.

"So do I," said Max. "Quit."

"Quit? We can't quit now, when
you've got things going so well!" said
Morry. "I've got a great idea! Let's go
over to the pond!"

"The pond? But —"

"Sure! It's a nice level place, with plenty of room."

"And plenty of water, too. Now, listen, Morry —"

"It's not deep and it's probably frozen. Even if it isn't, that won't matter, because the balloons will take you all the way across, easy!"

"How do you know?" said Max. "And it's a long way across."

"It's not more than twice as far as it is from the porch to this tree," said Morry. "Don't worry, you can make it, *easy*!"

Max frowned.

"Well," he said, "I'll walk over and take a look — but I'm not saying I'll do it."

Max and Morry headed for the pond.

Suddenly they heard shouts of "Help! Help!"

First it was one voice. Then they heard more voices.

"Help! Help!"

"What's that?" asked Max.

"I don't know," said Morry. "Come on, let's run!"

Several boys and girls stood in the snow at the edge of the ice. They were yelling excitedly and pointing out toward the middle of the pond. One boy had a piece of rope. He was trying to throw an end of the rope out onto the ice.

A boy had fallen through the ice. He splashed and kicked, holding onto the edge of the ice, where it had broken under him.

"Help! I'm freezing!" he shouted.

"What happened?" cried Morry.

"Jimmie Dugan went out on his skates to try the ice," said the boy with the rope, "but it wasn't solid. And I can't throw the rope far enough!"

Morry turned to Max. "Here! Blow this up!" he said, giving Max a balloon. "You can take the rope to Jimmie!"

"Who, me?" said Max.

"Yes! Hurry!"

Quickly they blew up the balloons. The others watched, too scared and

worried to do anything but stare at
them.

Max blew until he was out of breath,
and Morry was red-faced again, but the
balloons were full. Morry cried out,
"All set! Here's the end of the rope.
Take hold of it, Max, and keep hold of
the tube. Don't let go of the tube."

It was not easy. In one hand Max
had to hold both the rope and a tube.

"Don't jump too high," Morry
whispered. "If you do, it will look
funny."

Max nodded and frowned, getting
his will power going.

"Okay!" he said.

"Go!" said Morry.

Max made a small jump into the air,
so small that he skimmed away hardly
an inch above the ice. He seemed to be
running on the ice, half hidden by the
balloons bulging
in front of him.
Hands twisted
behind him
and elbows

sticking out at his sides, Max went
straight for the middle of the pond.

Morry stood on the edge worrying.
He waited till Max whizzed alongside
Jimmie and then yelled, "Drop it, Max!"

Max dropped the rope. But in his excitement he also dropped one balloon rocket.

Now he was like a jet airplane flying on one engine, only worse. He swung in a wide curve toward the side of the pond, but he needed more power. One balloon was not enough

Max moved slower and slower. He tried to run, but his legs only thrashed in the air. He tumbled sideways and hit the ice.

Crack! It broke under him and he crashed through into the water.

"Max! I'm coming!" cried Morry. He started running around the side of the pond as fast as he could run, which was not very fast. But before Morry had run far, Max stood up.

He was in shallow water, only up to his knees.

Morry was there in time to meet Max when he waded ashore, breaking ice all the way.

"Are you all right?" asked Morry.

"At-choo!" sneezed Max.

They looked back and saw that
Jimmie had caught hold of the rope.
The other boys and girls had pulled
him onto the ice and were dragging
him toward shore.

"You're a hero!" said Morry.

"I'm f-freezing!" said Max. His teeth
chattered loudly and he was shivering.

"Come on, you've got to get home!"
said Morry. "Think about being hot, or
you'll catch a cold!"

So they hurried home, with Max
frowning hard.

"Think hot, Max!" said Morry.
"Hot, hot, hot!"

Soon Max was thinking so hard
about being hot that his wet clothes
began to steam. A cloud of steam
formed around him and then spread to
Morry. It almost hid them from sight
as they raced along the street.

"Max, I've got a great idea!" cried Morry.

"No!" cried Max. "I don't want to hear anything about it!"

But then he stopped running.

"Well . . . what is it?" he asked. "Tell me about it — but that doesn't mean I'll do it!"